Cuddle Bear

Claire Freedman

Gavin Scott

Kane Miller
A DIVISION OF EDC PUBLISHING

If you feel a little sad,
Or lonely, lost and blue,
Don't worry, call for Cuddle Bear...

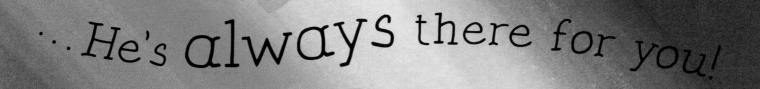

...He's **always** there for you!

Do you need cuddles, cheer-up hugs,
Or snuggle times to share?
Then Cuddle Bear is made for you –
A hug-you-happy bear!

This panda needs a
cuddle NOW!
She's tripped and
had a fright,

So Cuddle Bear

comes scooting up...

A **hug** will put things right.

Poor Penguin's
missing all her friends,
Alone and far away,

But not too far
for Cuddle Bear

To bring a hug –
HOORAY!

The animals are scared of Lion,
He looks so big and wild.

He's **never**,
ever had a hug,
That's why he's
never smiled.

"We all need hugs!" says Cuddle Bear,
"However fierce we look."
Now Lion's happy as can be.
One hug was all it took!

Next Little Rabbit wants a hug,

A happy, bouncy one!

A squishy-squashy-squeezy hug
Is super cuddly fun!

It really doesn't matter,
If you're

BIG...

or short...

...or tall,

"A hug from me," says Cuddle Bear,
"Will stretch to fit you all!"

"The world needs hugs!" says Cuddle Bear,
"To make each day feel bright.
So stretch both arms and wrap them round
your friends to hug them tight!"

So now you know the secret!
Here's what you have to do...

Just hug the person that you love,
And they will hug you, too!

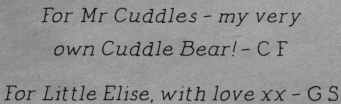

For Mr Cuddles - my very
own Cuddle Bear! - C F

For Little Elise, with love xx - G S

First American Edition 2012
Kane Miller, A Division of EDC Publishing

Text copyright © Claire Freedman 2012
Illustrations copyright © Gavin Scott 2012

For information contact:
Kane Miller, A Division of EDC Publishing
5402 S 122nd E Ave
Tulsa, OK 74146
www.kanemiller.com
www.myubam.com

Library of Congress Control Number: 2011933991
Printed in China
16 18 20 19 17

ISBN: 978-1-61067-081-4
LTP/1800/4050/0821